For Lucy

A DAVID FICKLING BOOK

Published by David Fickling Books
an imprint of Random House Children's Books
a division of Random House, Inc.
1540 Broadway
New York, New York 10036

Published simultaneously in Canada by Random House of Canada Limited, Toronto. Originally published in Great Britain by David Fickling Books, an imprint of Random House Children's Books.

www.randomhouse.com/kids

Library of Congress Cataloging-in-Publication Data available upon request.

ISBN 0-385-75014-5 (trade)

Printed in Singapore

August 2003

10 9 8 7 6 5 4 3 2 1

First American Edition

Pants

Giles Andreae
Nick Sharratt

David Fickling Books

OXFORD · NEW YORK

Small pants, big pants

Giant frilly pig pants

New pants, blue pants one, two, three

Loose pants, tight pants

Lighting up at night pants

no pants at all!

Pants to pick a daisy, pants for being lazy

Pants on your head
when you've gone crazy!

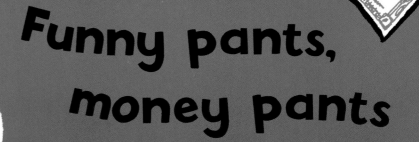

Funny pants,
money pants

Wear them when it's sunny pants

Have you seen these bunny pants?

Little baby nappy pants

Special pants for driving in the car!

Fairy pants, hairy pants

What a lot of lovely